A HAPPY ENDING BOOK ™

Moving Day

by Jane Carruth   illustrated by Tony Hutchings

MODERN PUBLISHING
A Division of Unisystems, Inc.
New York, New York 10022

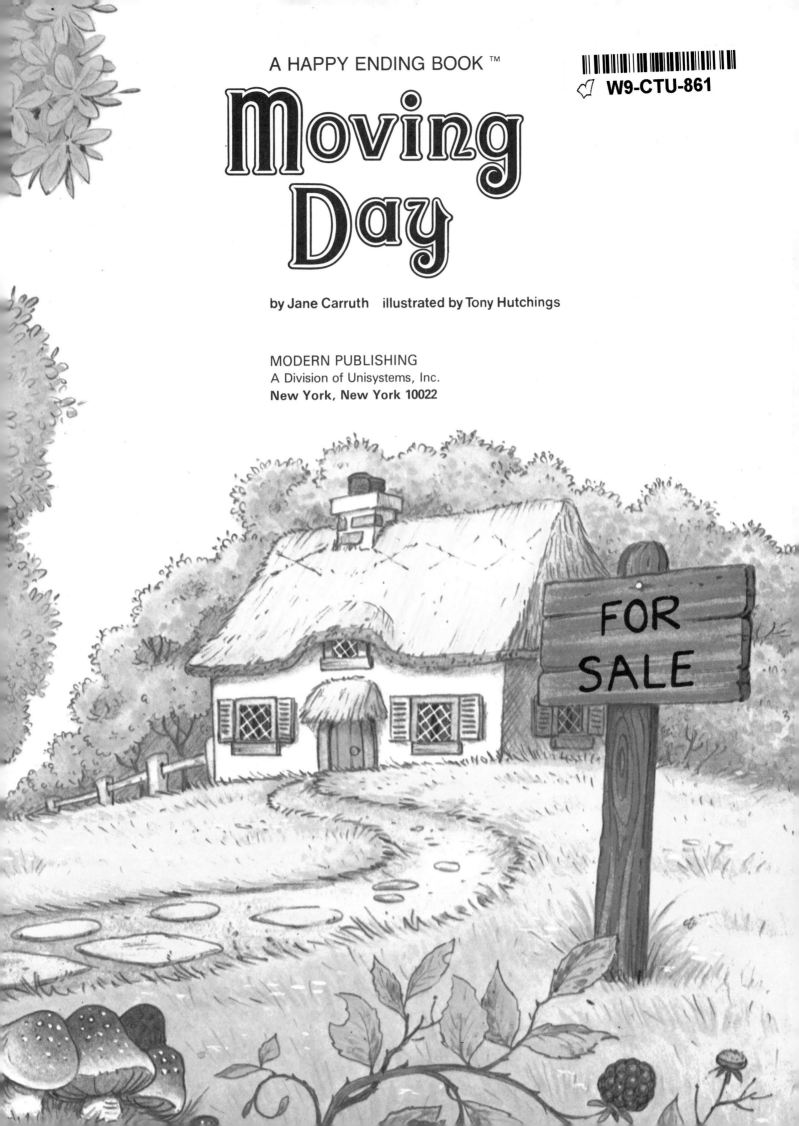

Hoppity was in the kitchen playing with his favorite toy, Tufty, when Sam Weasel popped his head through the open window to speak to Hoppity's mother.

"Is it all right to put the FOR SALE sign in the garden?" he asked.

"What sign?" Hoppity squeaked, nearly dropping Tufty.

"We're moving," Mommy told him, "so that we can be nearer to the place where Daddy works."

Hoppity was very upset when Mr. and Mrs. Bunkins
came the next week to look over the house. He hugged
Tufty and scowled at them through the bannisters.
But that didn't stop them from wanting to buy.
"We can move in very soon," they said.

That night, at supper, Daddy and Hoppity's big brother, Bobtail, heard the good news. They were very pleased. But poor little Hoppity was so miserable that he couldn't finish his supper. He didn't want to move to another house. He didn't want to lose all his friends.

On moving day, Daddy took time off from work to help. Bobtail didn't go to school. What hard work it was loading up the truck with all the carpets and the furniture and the pots and pans!

They were so busy they did not see little Hoppity run away into the woods all by himself.

Bobtail was the first to notice that his little brother was missing.

"Oh dear!" said Mommy anxiously. "Now where can he be hiding? I just don't know."

"I think I know," Bobtail cried. "I'm sure he has run off into the woods with Tufty!"

It didn't take Bobtail very long to find Hoppity.
"Come on!" he called. "And cheer up! Moving is
fun. And we'll soon make lots of new friends."
"I-I d-don't want to move," Hoppity sobbed.

After the move, Mommy began arranging the furniture in the new house. Then she climbed on a stool to fix some curtains. Bobtail said, "Let me help! I do like this house— it's even nicer than the old one!"

Mommy wished Hoppity would put Tufty down and start to put away his toys. But Hoppity kept on sitting in his little chair and looking miserable.

The next day, while shopping, Hoppity's mother was delighted to meet an old friend.

"What a surprise!" she exclaimed. "I didn't know we were neighbors. And this must be Sophie!"

Sophie tried to make friends with Hoppity.
"Will you let me hold your dolly?" she asked.
"Tufty is not a dolly!" Hoppity replied angrily.
"Don't touch him!" And he turned his back on her.

That afternoon Sophie and her little friends came to play with Hoppity.

"If you play," she said to Hoppity, "we can have two teams for tug-of-war. I'll be the referee."

Hoppity's favorite game was tug-of-war, so he had to join in. And he tugged so hard that he was sure he was helping his side to win!

After the game, Hoppity's mother said that they could
all come inside for sandwiches and cupcakes.
"Which side won?" she asked.
"My team was the strongest!" Hoppity laughed.
"I tugged and tugged. It was so much fun!"

Before it was time to go home, Hoppity showed Sophie
his new room and all his toys.

"I love Tufty best," said Sophie.

"So do I," said Hoppity, and he smiled happily.

Hoppity was busy drawing a picture of his new house with Sophie in it as well, when Daddy and Bobtail came home. "It's for Sophie," he told them. "And when she comes tomorrow she can have old Tufty too. I'm really too big for him now!"